W9-DES-275

*To everyone who has lost a tooth and to the innocent child in all of us. May all of your dreams come true!*

The Magic Sceptre TM
Teena the Tiny Tooth Fairy©
Text and Illustrations

Printed in China

For information address
Silver Snowflake Publishing.
P.O. Box 1256, East Greenwich, RI 02818
www.TheMagicSceptre.com
First Edition
1 3 5 7 10 8 6 4 2
SAN: 8 5 0 - 3 9 4 X
LCCN 2010909776

Publisher's Cataloging-in-Publication
(Provided by Quality Books, Inc.)

Creamer, Joan Klatil, 1943-
The magic sceptre : Teena the tiny tooth fairy / written and illustrated by Joan Klatil Creamer.
p. cm.
SUMMARY: Teena the Tiny Tooth Fairy is smaller than the other tooth fairies. The magic sceptre gives her just the right "tools" to help her be a successful fairy even though she is small.
Audience: Ages 4-8.
ISBN-13: 978-0-9778476-4-8
ISBN-10: 0-9778476-4-0

1. Tooth Fairy (Legendary character)--Juvenile fiction. 2. Stature--Juvenile fiction. 3. Success--Juvenile fiction. [1. Tooth Fairy--Fiction. 2. Size --Fiction. 3. Success--Fiction.] I. Title.
II. Title: Teena the tiny tooth fairy.

PZ7.C85985Mat 2010 [E]
QBI10-600134

# The Magic Sceptre

# Teena the Tiny Tooth Fairy

For Hannah
Remember the Magic!
Joan Klatil Creamer

Written and Illustrated by
Joan Klatil Creamer

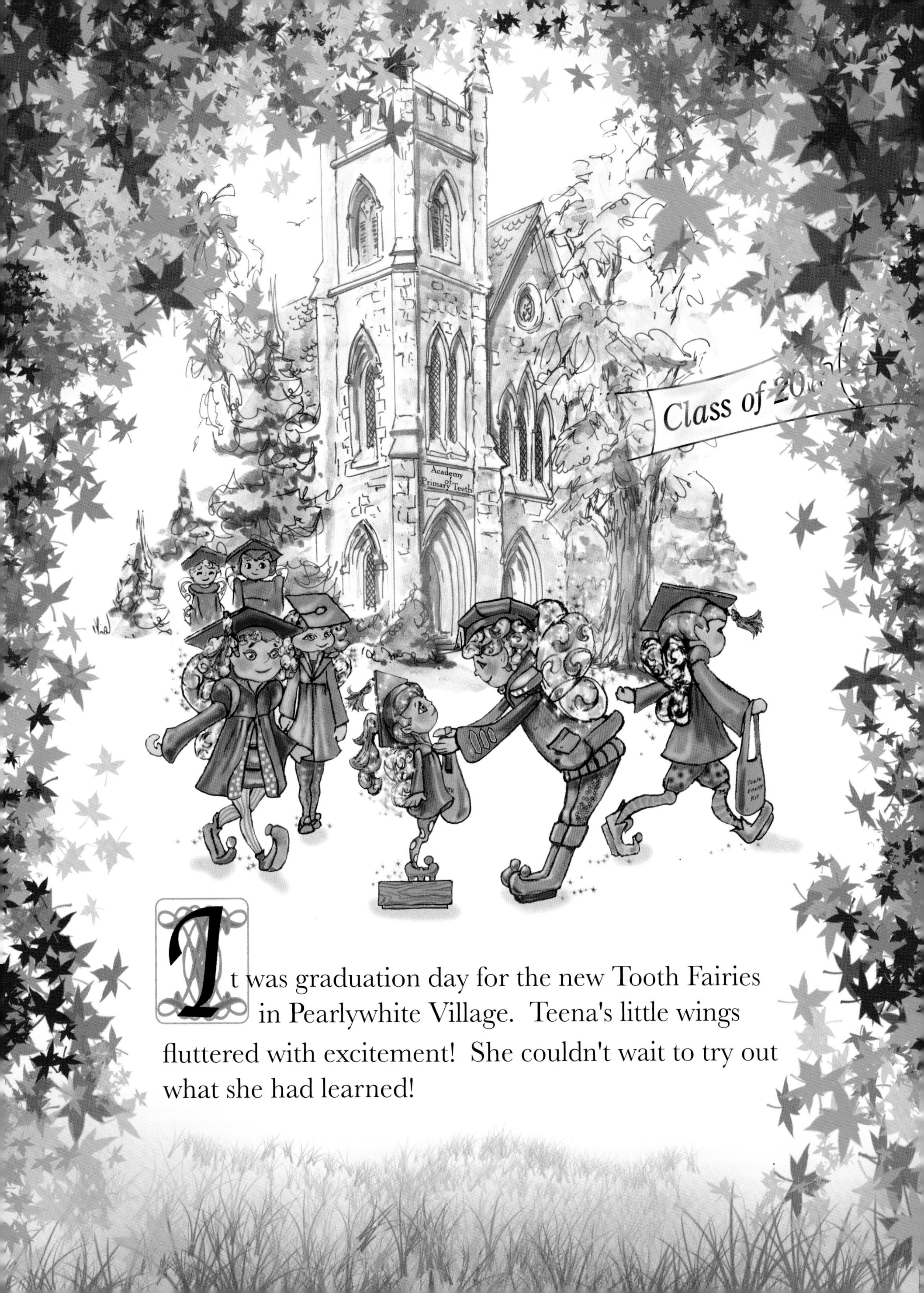


It was graduation day for the new Tooth Fairies in Pearlywhite Village. Teena's little wings fluttered with excitement! She couldn't wait to try out what she had learned!

"I've always dreamed of being a Tooth Fairy," she told the other graduates. "I know I'm small, but I can do it!"

After Teena received her Tooth Fairy Wing Pin and Tooth Fairy Kit, Tony, an experienced Tooth Fairy said to her, "Teena, don't forget, sometimes we run into problems because animals can hear and see ALL fairies, so we have to be QUICK!"

Teena remembered her days at The Academy of Primary Teeth.

They were taught to listen carefully for the BUZZING sound of a loose tooth and to look for the special GLOW of a tooth, even if it is hidden deep under the pillow. They also had to attend Wing Tip Flight School.

Teena also learned about The Command Center of Detached Teeth where names of children who have lost a tooth are printed each day.

CHRISTI
JEFFREY
GINNIE
SHAENA
JIM
MICHELLE
SALLY
PENNY
KYLE
HANNAH
MICHAEL
JOSEPH
ALICIA
TAYLA
JACK
WILL
MARISSA
MEGAN
CHRISTINE
JULIA
JULIA ANNE
KENDRA
LOGAN
SHANTELL
MARCO
DEE
HENRY
TED
RICHARD
VONNIE
DICK
FAYE
CHUCK
LINDA
CARRIE
ADAM
STEWART BEAU
LANCE
BOBBIE
SCOTT
BETH
AUDRA
TRISTAN
BRAD
BOB
JOYCE
TODD
MAUREEN
GAIL
DENNIS
DENISE
TYLER
PEARL
HELEN
CRAIG
CAMERON
FRED
STACEY
DEIRDRE
JAYDEN
GARRICK
BRENDEN
HANNAH
KERIANNE
KAITLYN
DANIEL
ERIKA
KEITH
JON
JENNIFER
CHASE
CASSIDY
PAYTON
EVAN
AUDREY
BILL
PATSY
PHIL
JACKIE
JEFF
TYLER
PETER
PHOEBE
JODIE
FRAN
TOM
MICKI
MITCHEL
SUE
DAN
HOLLY
SHAYNA
JUDE
RAEGAN
ANDREA
LORI
LEAH
LIAM
KRICKIE
JONATHON
WILL
DONNA
MADDIE
DENNIS
PATTI
PATTY
GLENN
MARSHA
LARRY
JUDE
JOHN
JANIE
PAIGE
CARLY
GRIFFIN
SYDNEY
JORDAN
JILLIAN
EMILY
LENA
GULIANNA
STEVEN
JAYNE
NORMA
AIDEN
KAIYA
LILLY
ROBERT
CLARE
WYATT
MAX
CONNIE
BUD
ANNE
BOB
JULIE
MARNIE
JENNA
JESSICA
JOHN
OWEN
ISABELLA
ROCCO
JERRY
PAULINE
BARBARA
MARSHALL
HARRISON
LORRAINE
KEENAN
EINSTEIN
KARSON
LORENZO
CONNOR
CHRISTOPHER
SARAH
DOLORES
BRENDA
ABIGAIL
JESSY
BRIAN
COOPER
JOEY
CARLY
LILLY
ABIGAIL
MEREDITH
SUNNY
CORIE
KIRA
BRADEN
RICHARD
WILLIAM
DONALD
SUZANNE
LAUREN
GENE
ALYCE
LOGAN
HUNTER
KARA
PATRICK
MATT
JESSE
WYATT
JESSICA
AIDAN
ASHLEY
ALEXANDRIA
SAMANTHA
EMILY
CHERYL
FERGUS
LORAN
CHAD
TOM
ELAINE
CHARLIE
JULIA
KAREN
CHUCK
MARK
LORI
ARIELLE
BRAD
COREY
SHANA
ROGER
PATTI
LAURIE
JUSTIN
JASON
GINNY
NORMAN
SHEILA
NORMAN
NOAH
CATHY
TOM
TILL
BUCK
CAROLINE
SYDNEY
ZACHARY
AMBER
SUMMER
FELICITY
ASHELYNN
SUNNY
TANNER
KILEY
BRIANA
ALICYN
JUSTIN

Now it was time for Teena to receive her list of names and to start her journey along with the other fairies that were receiving their lists.

RETURN TEETH AREA
W
S
N
E
JOAN
BAILEY
MORRIS
BUDDY
KITCH
ROCCO
KIRA
JOYCE
PAUL
MICHAEL
EVAN
TAYLA
ELIZABETH
HARRY
JERRY
JESSICA
MADISON
STEWART

"Hmmmm, this is going to be tricky," she said, as she collected her first tooth.

The second tooth was a little more of a problem. It had slipped out from under the pillow and was near his nose. Teena was able to get it without waking him. "Whew! I did it, even though I am small!"

The third tooth glowed brightly, but when she put the tooth in her bag, Megan's dog woke up. This was quite a challenge.

TOMMY, the next name on the list, had a question mark after it. What did this mean?

When she arrived at his house for the fourth tooth, she saw it was rather large. As she got closer, Teena saw it was a "glow in the dark" tooth box as big as Teena. She struggled to open it.

Inside was a small candy that LOOKED like a tooth. Tommy wanted to be like his older brother, Bill, who recently lost a tooth.

"Do all fairies have this problem with pens or pencils," she wondered?

Just then her Sunrise Alert Watch started beeping! "Oh no!
It's the first ray of morning sunshine! Fairies are visible in the first
light of day."

TEETH
Sunrise
ACCIDENTALLY BROKEN TEETH NOT READY
TEETH TO BE CLEANED & POLISHED
TEETH READY TO BE MADE INTO DISTANT STARS

Teena was tired from gathering the first 3 teeth. The bag was now too heavy; she couldn't get off the ground. She was the last to arrive at the Command Center, dragging the bag behind her. The other fairies tried hard not to laugh.

The next evening, Teena had only ONE name on her list.

She started her journey north...WAY up north. Finally looking down, she saw an unusual house. In addition to the BUZZING and GLOW of the tooth, she heard the JINGLING of sleigh bells. "Oh my." Teena's wings shook with excitement, "It's Santa's Village!"

A little elf had lost his first tooth. Just as she was about to leave with the tooth, she saw the most beautiful snowflake. "Wow!" she whispered to herself. "How could I have forgotten, Santa gets ALL his work done in one night. I'm sure he could help me."

by
ELDRED
ELDRED
The Magic Sceptre
TEDDY
DEAR TOOTH FAIRY
TONIGHT I LOST

Teena timidly tapped on Santa's door...no answer. She knocked a little louder...still no answer. Then, with all her might, she pounded again.

"I almost didn't hear or see you there Teena," said Santa, his belly shaking as he laughed.

Santa invited her to sit down. Teena told Santa all the problems she was having.

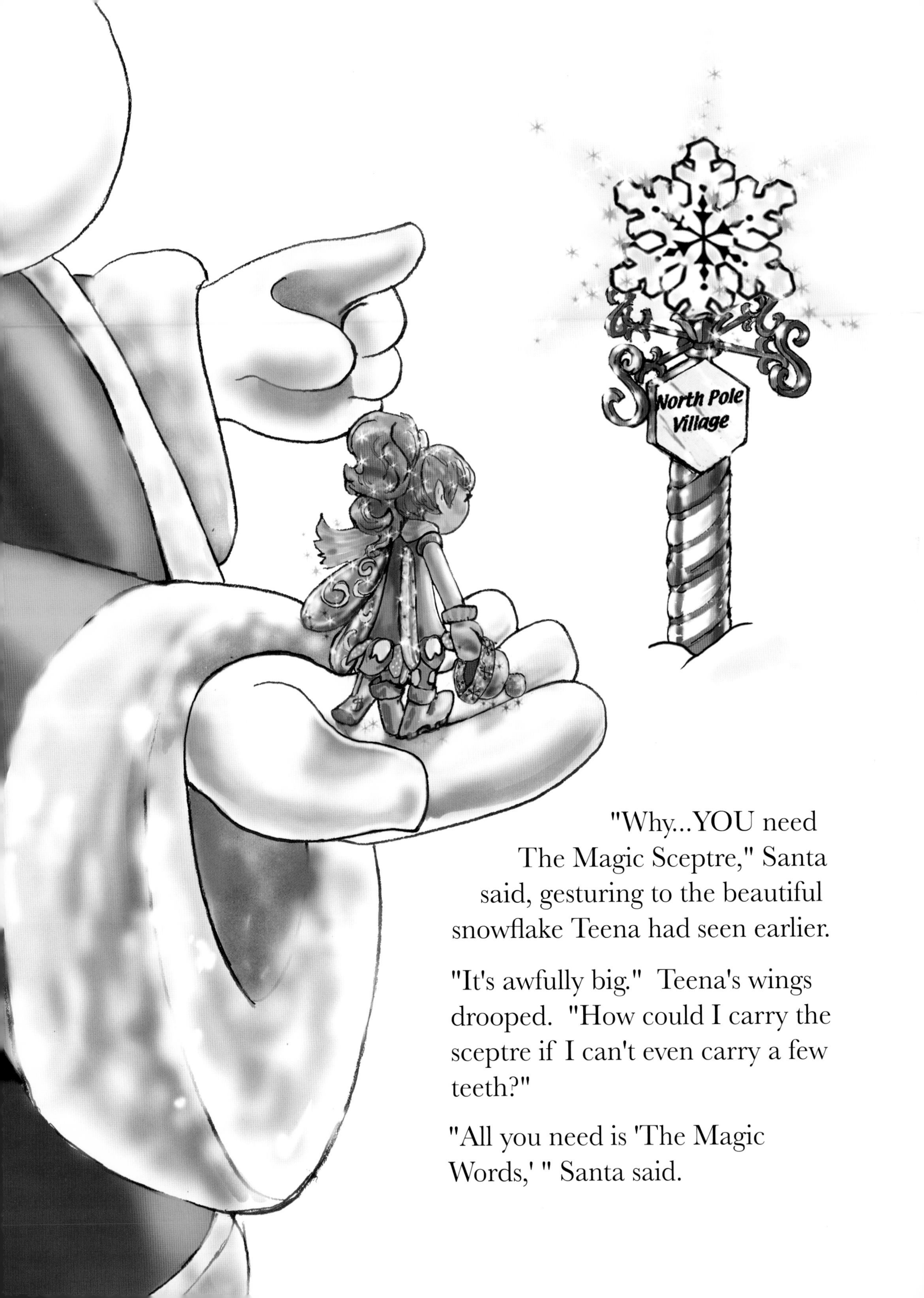


"Why...YOU need The Magic Sceptre," Santa said, gesturing to the beautiful snowflake Teena had seen earlier.

"It's awfully big." Teena's wings drooped. "How could I carry the sceptre if I can't even carry a few teeth?"

"All you need is 'The Magic Words,' " Santa said.

Teena repeated after Santa,
**"Believe in the Magic and all that it brings, the Sceptre will be there to do just the right things"**...and POOF!!!

Many magical bags of dust came into sight. Even a twirling magic pen appeared that writes when spoken to.

When Teena put the collected teeth into the new bag, they were so light the bag almost carried her away.

On cold nights, Teena took swirling rides on a snowflake snowboard that was just the right size for an extra tiny Tooth Fairy. On warm summer evenings she rode on a cute little firefly.

Sprinkling Magic Dust on the puppy's nose made him move in slow motion, allowing Teena to get the tooth and leave a present.

One fall evening, Teena was returning to the Command Center when she saw many of her fellow tooth fairies below. She decided to see what was happening.

One of the teeth had fallen through a hole in a tooth fairy bag and into a storm drain just out of reach of any of the Tooth Fairies' fingertips.The water level was rising; soon the tooth would be lost forever. Acting quickly, Teena was able to squeeze through the grating and retrieve the tooth, a very brave and scary act that only a small fairy could do. Teena saved the tooth just in time.

The Tooth Fairies never laughed at Teena again for being so tiny.

She returned The Magic Sceptre to the North Pole and asked that every tooth fairy be given a small magic wand. Now all the Tooth Fairies could have even more Magic, just like Teena's.

So, if you see a firefly or beautiful snowflake shooting by at dusk, perhaps Teena, the Tiny Tooth Fairy, is on her way to collect the teeth of the children on her list, and leave money or special gifts in their place.

Did you know that in France, the tooth fairy is called La Petite Souris? In Spanish speaking countries there is a magical little mouse called Ratoncito Perez that collects the children's teeth and in Italy his name is Topino.

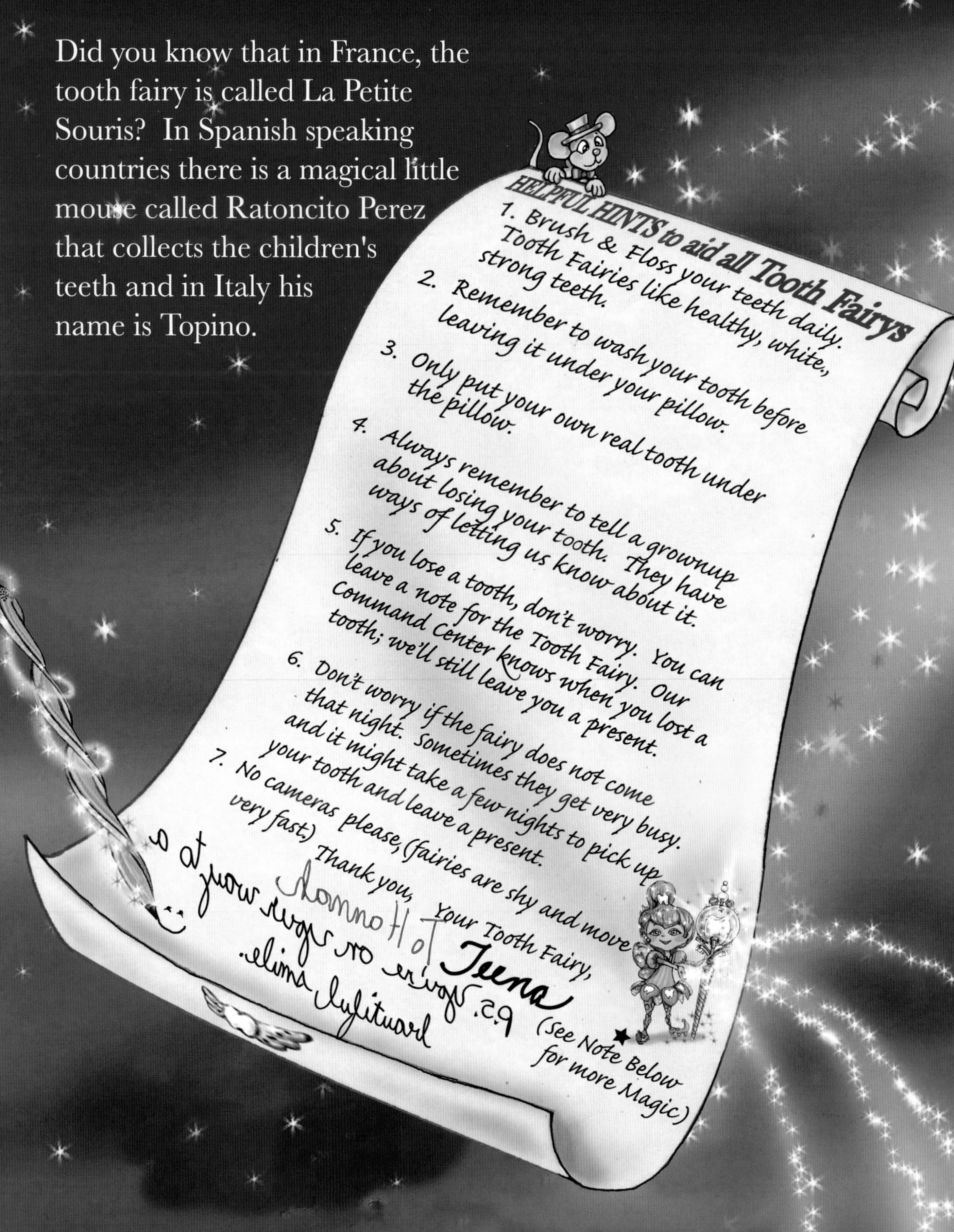


Hold this page up to a mirror to see more MAGIC! Teena will have a special message just for you!